Copyright © 2019 by Gavin Aung Than
Original interior design by Gavin Aung Than and
Benjamin Fairclough © Penguin Random House Australia Pty Ltd.

All rights reserved. Published in the United States by Random House Children's Books,
a division of Penguin Random House LLC, New York. Originally published by Puffin Books,
an imprint of Penguin Random House Australia Pty Ltd., Sydney, in 2019.

Random House and the colophon are registered trademarks of Penguin Random House LLC.

RH Graphic with the book design is a trademark of Penguin Random House LLC.

Visit us on the Web! rhcbooks.com

Educators and librarians, for a variety of teaching tools,
visit us at RHTeachersLibrarians.com

Library of Congress Cataloging-in-Publication Data is available upon request.
ISBN 978-0-593-17512-5 (trade pbk.)
ISBN 978-0-593-17509-5 (hardcover)
ISBN 978-0-593-17510-1 (lib. bdg.)
ISBN 978-0-593-17511-8 (ebook)

The artist used Adobe Photoshop to create the illustrations for this book.
The text of this book is set in 11-point Sugary Pancake.
This edition's cover and interior design by Sylvia Bi and colorization by Sarah Stern

MANUFACTURED IN CHINA
10 9 8 7 6 5 4 3 2 1
First American Edition

BOOK TWO

SUPER SIDE KICKS

OCEAN'S REVENGE

Gavin Aung Than

Color by Sarah Stern

Random House New York

PREVIOUSLY...

Four superhero sidekicks were sick of being bullied
by their selfish grown-up partners, so they decided
to form their own team. They are the...

SUPER SIDEKICKS!

JUNIOR JUSTICE

Born leader. Expert martial artist. Brilliant detective.
Assisted by Ada, the world's most advanced belt buckle.

FLYGIRL

Acrobatic flyer. Bug whisperer. Cricket lover (the sport and
the insect). Uses dangerous bug balls to subdue enemies.

DINOMITE

Dinosaur shape-shifter. Physics professor. Poetry
connoisseur. Would rather be reading a book.

GOO

Limitless stretch factor. Untapped power potential.
Still has nightmares about his past as a bad guy.

THE GROWN-UPS

Captain Perfect, the world's most beloved
(and obnoxious) superhero; Rampagin'
Rita, simple yet scary strong; and Blast
Radius, who hasn't met a problem he
couldn't solve by blowing it up.

Chapter

Welcome, fearless readers.

It's great to have you back for another thrilling Super Sidekicks adventure!

Our story begins here, in the pristine blue waters of the Pacific Ocean.

But if you look a little closer, you'll see that the waters are not so pristine.

They are, in fact, **littered** with trash— **OUR** trash.

Millions of tons of the world's junk end up here . . .

. . . the Great Pacific Garbage Patch.

A giant whirlpool of garbage soup the size of a small country.

And what makes up most of it?

Plastic, plastic, and **more plastic!**

Plastic that has invaded the ecosystem.

Plastic that wreaks havoc on marine wildlife.

Plastic that will never, **ever** go away.

But what's this? Something strange is happening. The plastic trash seems to be joining together . . .

It's miraculously combining to form **bigger and bigger** pieces.

Some strange force is pulling millions of plastic pieces together in a swirling, hypnotic trash ballet.

At last, all of the trash from the Great Pacific Garbage Patch has been concentrated into one giant **plastic super cluster.**

The island crackles and pops with a violent energy.

Wait. It can't be.

It's not possible! The plastic island . . . it . . .

9

WHAM!

—away with this.

SCHLOOP!

All over the world, Earth's other superheroes are also being taken out.

Star Knight is the next to go.

Mother Bear gets surprised while on vacation in Siberia.

Sir Bucky Buckingham
doesn't stand a chance
against this mysterious foe.

Heroine **Bellatrix**
gets taken while flying
over the Amazon River.

Old Man Dragon falls prey to the tentacle attack.

And finally, **Lucie Liberté** gets dragged into the sewer system!

18

And just like that, the planet's first line of defense is gone . . .

MISSING

Superheroes of Earth

CAPTAIN PERFECT

RAMPAGIN' RITA

BLAST RADIUS

STAR KNIGHT

MOTHER BEAR

SIR BUCKY BUCKINGHAM

BELLATRIX

OLD MAN DRAGON

LUCIE LIBERTÉ

Who will protect us now?

Chapter

May I ask why you're fascinated by them?

Just between you and me, Ada, **clowns give me the creeps.**

Sifu* taught me one should **always face fear head-on.** The more I train against clowns, the less scared I get.

* A Cantonese word meaning "martial arts teacher."

Is it working?

Yeah, I think I'm making some real . . .

AHHH!

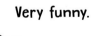

I'll reset the same opponents for tomorrow, shall I?

Very funny.

Well, "beautiful" is when something is nice-looking. A person can be beautiful on the **inside**, too.

Or when something is just soooooo pretty it makes you feel all **warm** and **fuzzy** inside. Mmm, like a **Goliath bird-eating spider**.

Like Flygirl. Flygirl beautiful!

Aw, thanks, you **beautiful** pink blob!

Why Flygirl teach Goo reading?

'Cause you need to be a good reader to learn about, well . . . **everything!**

Books are filled with all the knowledge in the world. You need some of that since you're not a prisoner in Dr. Enok's lab anymore.*

* Goo was created by the evil Dr. Enok. As seen in Super Sidekicks book 1!

Yay! **Knowww-led-ge**

And books can be full of **amazing** stories that transport you to **fantastical** places where you get to meet **incredible** characters!

Whoooaaaa.

Thank you for helping Goo. Goo happy here. Goo happy to be **Super Sidekick.**

Me too, mate. Me too.

GULP

I've been looking for him **everywhere!**

Lucky you didn't chew on him, JJ. Giant centipedes are pretty feisty. My mate Sebastian here would have given your tongue a nasty bite.

How many times do I have to tell you, Flygirl? Please, **PLEEEASE,** keep your door closed.

SLURP!

None of us want to accidentally eat one of your **gross bugs!**

MUNCH MUNCH

Isn't that right, Goo?

Mmm—hmm.

IT'S READY!

The **SSSDSC** scans the world for all possible threats, and alerts us to what needs our immediate attention. It's a triumph of **computer risk analysis.**

This feels like the final piece our team has been waiting for. Now we're ready for our **first official mission.**

THE SUPER SIDEKICKS ARE READY TO SAVE THE—

Does this thing have TV?

Ah, here we go.

I'm here at Sydney Tower for the eighteenth annual **Very Important Summit . . .**

... where the world's most powerful leaders have gathered to discuss pressing global issues. They will be working together to solve urgent problems threatening our planet.

Of course, we don't know the exact details of these talks, but I can assure you ... they're very, very, **VERY** important.

Bah, these summits are a waste of time!

I used to work as security at these things with Captain Perfect, and **nothing ever got solved.** The leaders just spent the whole time arguing about who had the **best golf swing.**

That's odd. I don't see Captain Perfect there.

Also missing are all the other superheroes who act as their leader's bodyguards. Strange. **Very strange indeed.**

SUPER-DUPER ALERT! SUPER-DUPER ALERT!

The computer— it's found something!

Chapter

What about communication? We can't talk down there.

Allow me to assist.

I can provide a mental link between the four of you while underwater.

KA-KLA

Connection complete.

You can now communicate with each other using your thoughts.

SCHURLLLP

POP!

GOOspeed!

Yuck, they're everywhere.

Your species is **spectacularly** shortsighted. The plastic humans produce takes hundreds, sometimes **thousands,** of years to decompose. Just because you throw it away doesn't mean it magically disappears.

I didn't think it was this bad.

Naughty humans. **Naughty!**

We should be approaching the threat soon. **Still no visual.**

WHOA!

The water's getting choppy!

I can't see anything.

It's so dark all of a sudden.

59

I repeat: **evacuate immediately!** This is not a drill.

See for yourself if you don't believe me!

AHHHHHHHHH!!!

Ada, megaphone mode. **NOW!**

Voice amplification ready.

THIS IS *JUNIOR JUSTICE.* TELL US WHAT YOU *WANT.* THERE ARE *INNOCENT* PEOPLE HERE!

STOP!

Goo your friend! Tell Goo what friend want!

PLEASE!

GRKK?

Chapter

THUD!

We're . . . we're still alive!

What is this place?

Hee hee hee.

Distinguished guests, allow me to introduce myself . . .

Mrs. Prime Minister, is that you?!

Captain Perfect! Star Knight, Mother Bear . . . My goodness, **you're all here!**

I'm sorry we couldn't protect you, ma'am.

Evil witch took Rita by surprise.

What about your super strength?

Can't you just break free?

YOU.

Us?

You are the ones who claim to be in **charge of this planet,** are you not?

Uh . . . I guess.

Yes, we are **very powerful!**

Good. That is why I brought you all here.

So I can see you sweat and try to squirm your way out of something from which there is **no escape.**

Because today is the day you will all be sentenced for your **crimes against the ocean!**

I thought no species would be careless enough to **destroy their own home.** Cutting down forests, wiping out animals, and burning the ancient fossils in the ground, which suffocates the planet!

Surely no species could be so reckless. **Surely** their leaders would do something about it. **Surely** they would work together to fix it. But year after year, **you did nothing.**

All you seemed to do was squabble and bicker among yourselves while my kingdom was **GETTING RUINED!**

So do you know what happened next?

Sydney is just the first of many cities to fall. My Titan was created with only the plastic in the **PACIFIC** Ocean.

There are millions more tons of your junk in my other oceans that can be turned into Titans.

More Titans to destroy all your hideous cities.

Ah, revenge is so much more satisfying than being patient!

You . . . you can't do this.

Tell me something, Mrs. Prime Minister . . .

. . . who's going to stop me?

Um . . . Goo have idea.

Heh.

Spit it out, mate.

Goo **friend** with plastic thing. Goo tell friend to **stop.**

It did seem to hesitate when you spoke to it.

But plastic friend distracted. Goo need try again. **Get closer.**

You do share similarities. Dr. Enok created you in a lab, and this creature seems to be some kind of artificial being . . .

It could be serving a master like you once did, Goo. Perhaps there is a **strange connection** between you.

What about Ada's **mental link thingy?** Would that help?

Good idea! Ada, can it be done?

In theory, yes. I can translate any language in the universe.

Though I would have to be placed in an **optimal position,** between the creature's eyes, for any chance of success.

We have to try!

It would be an exciting experiment in linguistics.

But how are we going to get Goo close enough?

WHO ... WHO ARE YOU?

Yay. Friend understand. **Me Goo.** Friend have name?

MOTHER CALLS ME TITAN. TRASH TITAN.

Mmm, Goo think **Trevor** better name. Friend like?

TREVOR? YES. I DO. BUT MOTHER WOULD NOT.

Heck no. You can sit this one out if you like, buddy.

Sigh.

FHOOF!

To quote Shakespeare: **"Once more unto the breach, dear friends."**

I don't know what that means, but we stick together. **Always.**

Goo ready!

Well, gang, if we don't make it out of this alive, I just want to tell you that being your teammate has been totally . . .

Chapter

I AM SORRY, MOTHER. MY FRIENDS WANT TO SPEAK TO YOU.

Hello!

... friends?

FRIENDS? WHAT...

JJ, you're hit!

I'm not that stressed, Flygirl.

See, I don't have any powers for this thing to feed on.

You're just . . . a **civilian?**

A civilian who's dedicated his life to mastering the martial arts . . .

POP!

TICKLE TICKLE

. . . including **Mongolian tickle fighting!**

STOP! STOP!

You should probably turn around now.

FHOOF!

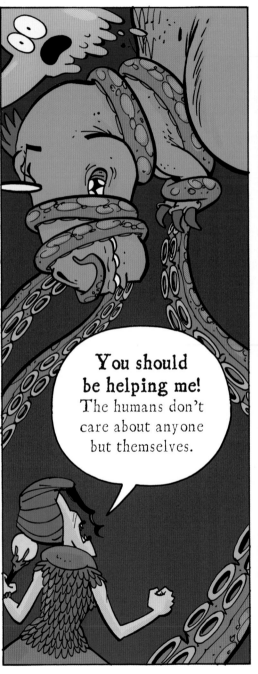

You should be helping me! The humans don't care about anyone but themselves.

SCHLONK!

FHOOF!

OW!

Can't transform! Blast this infernal Asteroidea*.

* That's the scientific term for "starfish."

99.9% probability of scepter's position acquired. Throw your staff at my target with maximum strength ...

... in 4, 3, 2, 1.

LAUNCH!

Oh no! I didn't think she could climb like that!

Your audacity will cost you your life, little one.

Now give that—

You promise to stop the pollution? The plastic waste? The oil drilling?

We promise!

But I'm a shareholder in oil.

Shut up, Richard!

Why should **I believe them?** They've never lifted a finger before.

You said it yourself—we're children. **Our future depends on cleaning up the planet, too.** You have our word, ma'am.

Don't believe them. **Believe us!**

Very well.

You have **one year.** Or the Trash Titans will return.

Understood.

And I have one more condition. These world leaders must help with the cleaning themselves. **One hundred tons of plastic each.**

What?!

She can't be serious!

Can't my vice president do it?

DEAL!

Chapter

141

. . . and converts it into **clean energy**. Plastic can now replace fossil fuels as the planet's main energy source.

You're a genius, Dinomite!

Bravo!

If this doesn't win me the Nobel Prize, nothing will.

Don't worry, the Super Sidekicks
will be back in

SUPER SIDE KICKS

BOOK THREE

TRIAL OF HEROES

The Super Sidekicks just saved the world and got invited to join
H.E.R.O.—the Heroic Earth Righteousness Organization—an exclusive club
for the planet's most famous superheroes. But before they can become
members, the team must pass the hardest challenge in the universe,
a test so scary and difficult only the truly heroic can survive.

COMING IN 2022!

Sounds like a
must-read!

THE PLANET NEEDS YOU!

THREE GREAT WAYS YOU CAN ELIMINATE WASTE—AND BE A HERO.

Waste, and how we choose to handle it, affects our environment. It has to be carefully controlled so it doesn't harm Earth or our health. You can help the planet by learning and practicing the three Rs of waste management:

Reduce: Buy and use less! If all the other people on Earth used as much "stuff" as we do in the United States, there would need to be three to five times more space just to hold and sustain everybody. WOW!

Reuse: You can "reuse" materials in their original form instead of throwing them away. Plastic cups, plates, and utensils can be washed and used again.

Recycle: Don't just toss everything in the trash! Lots of things can be remade into either the same kind of object or new products. Things that you can recycle include aluminum cans, cardboard, electronic equipment, glass, magazines, metal, plastic bags, and plastic bottles.

Thanks for the plastic-bottle punching bag!

TO LEARN MORE, VISIT
KIDS.NIEHS.NIH.GOV/TOPICS/REDUCE/

THE FUTURE OF THE PLANET IS IN YOUR . . . . LUNCH BOX?!

Did you know that a person creates an average of 4.5 pounds of trash per day? By reducing the number of items in your lunch that must be thrown out, you can:

→ **PREVENT POLLUTION**

→ **CONSERVE NATURAL RESOURCES**

→ **SAVE ENERGY**

→ **REDUCE THE NEED FOR DISPOSAL**

→ **BE AN ENVIRONMENTAL HERO AND MAKE A DIFFERENCE**

Practice the three Rs of waste management and work with your school administrators, teachers, and cafeteria staff to organize a Waste-Free Lunch Day. Encourage students to bring their lunch in reusable containers made of cloth, durable plastic, or glass. Work with the school cafeteria staff to plan a "waste-free lunch" for students who can't bring their own from home.

For a step-by-step guide on how to plan a Waste-Free Lunch Day, along with downloadable assets and other resources, visit epa.gov/students/pack-waste-free-lunch.

It's easy to reduce waste when you know Goo!

GAVIN'S DRAWING TIPS

START WITH SIMPLE SHAPES FIRST: For instance, Dinomite is mostly made of circles, rectangles, and triangles.

DON'T DRAW TOO DARK: Sketch lightly until you get the basic structure right.

ONE STEP AT A TIME: Once you have the structure done, it's time to draw all the cool details.

JUST HAVE FUN: Don't worry if you think you're not getting it right. Keep practicing—it takes time to get good!

DRAW DINOMITE

1.   2.   3.

DRAW GOO

1.   2.   3.

Gavin Aung Than is a *New York Times* bestselling cartoonist and the creator of the Super Sidekicks. Gavin grew up loving to draw superheroes and now, as an adult, gets to draw them for a living. He's sure this is some kind of mistake.

Visit Gav's website at AungThan.com and follow him on social media!